First American Edition 2004
by Kane/Miller Book Publishers, Inc.
La Jolla, California

Copyright © Sanne te Loo 2003
Originally published by Lemniscaat b.v. Rotterdam
All rights reserved. For information contact:
Kane/Miller Book Publishers
P.O. Box 8515
La Jolla, CA 92038
www.kanemiller.com

Library of Congress Control Number: 2003109284

Printed and Bound in China by Regent Publishing Services Ltd.

2 3 4 5 6 7 8 9 10

ISBN: 978-1-929132-59-1

Little Fish

Kane/Miller
BOOK PUBLISHERS

Rosa is bored. Grandmother is busy making tortillas for market.

"Come on, Esperanza," says Rosa, giving the donkey a push.

"Let's go play." But the donkey doesn't move.

Rosa goes to the beach by herself. She sits on a rock and looks out over the sea. With a big splash, the pelicans dive down into the water, and then come up again with their beaks full of fish. One little fish though, seems very smart and is very fast. Every time one of those big beaks nearly catches him, he jumps out of the water. "Quick, little fish!" Rosa cries. Whoosh! Suddenly, her skirt is soaking wet. What is that swimming in her lap? "Little Fish," Rosa says, amazed. "Don't be afraid. You are safe with me."

Rosa holds her skirt high and walks home very carefully.

When she gets there, Grandmother is just leaving for market with the tortillas. "Grandmother, Grandmother, look!" cries Rosa excitedly. "What a sweet little fish," Grandmother says. "You'd better give him something to eat."

Rosa puts her fish in a beautiful bowl filled with water, and then places it on the kitchen table. "I'll make you some crusty corn rolls," she tells Little Fish. "You're sure to love them." Soon there is a wonderful smell in the kitchen, which drifts outside the house. The boy who lives next door pokes his head in. "Mmmmm, Rosa, what a delicious smell!" "I am making my favorite rolls," Rosa tells him. "May I have one?" the little boy asks. Rosa shakes her head. "They are for Little Fish." When the rolls are finished baking, Little Fish starts to eat. He eats and eats until the very last roll is gone. With a fat belly and a contented sigh, he swims around his bowl.

The next morning, Rosa is woken up by a loud crash. The bowl has broken into pieces and Little Fish is lying on the kitchen floor. "Look how much you've grown since last night!" Rosa exclaims. "Quick, put him in this tub," Grandmother says. "He should fit in here."

Just for Little Fish, Rosa begins to cook all her favorite dishes. One day she makes a sweet cassava cake, the next day tortillas with lobster and cactus slices. Little Fish eats everything. The other children who live in the neighborhood come to have a look at Little Fish. "What a beautiful fish," they say, "and look how big he is getting!"

Yes, Rosa's fish is *growing*

and *growing*

and **growing**...

"He doesn't fit in the tub anymore," Grandmother says. "Why don't you put him outside in Esperanza's water trough?" What a good idea! Little Fish goes into the trough, and Rosa goes back inside to bake him a wonderful cake. Suddenly, she hears the little boy from next door shouting. "Rosa, Rosa, come quickly!" Rosa looks outside…

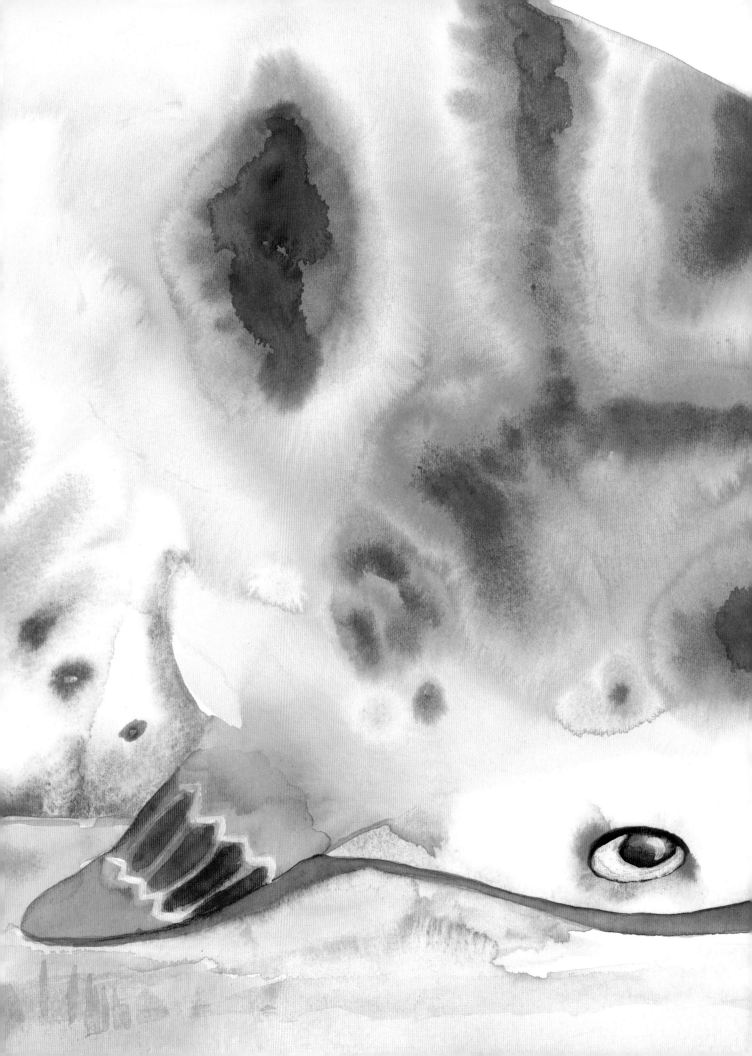

…and is shocked! Little Fish has grown some more! He is much too big for the trough, or for anywhere else.

"He must go back to the sea at once," Grandmother says.

Together, the children pick up Little Fish and carry him all the way

from Rosa's house…

...through the village...

…to the sea. There, they put him in the water. "You don't have to be afraid of the pelicans anymore," Rosa says, "but I will miss you." Little Fish splashes with his tail and dives under the water. "What a pity about the cake," Rosa sighs. "He didn't even have a chance to taste it." "Cake?" the other children shout. "There is cake? Hooray!!"

Grandmother has finished baking and decorating the cake.

Rosa cuts big pieces for everyone since there is plenty to share.

In the distance, Little Fish leaps out of the water. "Look," says

Rosa, "he looks just as little as the first time I saw him."